Thomas Magee

Three Essays

The Alphabet and Language, Immortality of the Big Trees, Wealth and Poverty of

the Chicago Exposition

Thomas Magee

Three Essays
The Alphabet and Language, Immortality of the Big Trees, Wealth and Poverty of the Chicago Exposition

ISBN/EAN: 9783743388673

Manufactured in Europe, USA, Canada, Australia, Japa

Cover: Foto ©Andreas Hilbeck / pixelio.de

Manufactured and distributed by brebook publishing software
(www.brebook.com)

Thomas Magee

Three Essays

The Alphabet and Language

Immortality of the Big Trees

Wealth and Poverty of the Chicago Exposition

Three Essays

By

Thomas Magee

WILLIAM DOXEY
631 MARKET STREET, UNDER PALACE HOTEL
SAN FRANCISCO
1895

PREFACE.

ANY ONE actuated by a proper spirit, who has derived great mental profit and pleasure from prolonged study of outdoor nature, or of art, science, or any branch of instructive literature, desires to extend that pleasure and profit to others. This will especially be true where a lover of good books constantly sees, from library reports, how small a proportion of such books are tasted beside the vast number of trashy volumes devoured. The writer of these essays knows that the subjects herein treated are great and profitable ones, and that, even if he has been incompetent to do anything like justice to them, or has misapprehended some of their teachings and laws, his book still contains enough instructive and elevating facts to attract the attention of students. He thereby hopes to lead them to pursue the study of some at least of the subjects herein directly or indirectly treated. He has derived intense pleasure and profit therefrom; others cannot fail to give like testimony, if they use like diligence.

The author has long been deeply impressed with the necessity of mental digestion and assimilation following reading. If they do not, reading is but unprofitable "cramming," from which no real mental nutriment is derived. He, therefore, urges students to *think* as they read, and to allow no author to impress his conclusions upon them until they have themselves carefully exercised their best judgment upon the subject under review.

CONTENTS.

The Alphabet and Language.

The Alphabet and Language.

HOMER, Æschylus, Sophocles, Euripides, Aristophanes, Dante, Shakespeare, and Milton have all produced works upon which the world has stamped the highest seal of approval; but a vastly greater and more difficult work preceded them, without which their authorship and fame would alike have been impossible. This work was the ALPHABET, the production of which was, in some respects, the greatest mental achievement ever accomplished by man. The knowledge of our A B C's, that begins almost when the maternal lacteal nourishment ends, and which in education bears about the same relation to solid knowledge that first nourishment does to solid food, is more wonderful to contemplate, and was more difficult and tedious of invention and perfection, than the works of the world's most deeply — revered authors. Individual men were the authors of our greatest books; but it required the three greatest nations of antiquity, and at least six thousand years of time, to produce a phonetic alphabet. And even then it had not by any means reached its present stage of development; for it is still far from perfection.

Even yet the alphabet does not by any means furnish a visible sign for every audible sound which the voice utters. It is both redundant and defective; of the twenty-six letters of our alphabet, three (*c*, *q*, and *x*) are practically useless, and we are therefore left with but twenty-three letters to express not less than thirty-two sounds. The phonetic alphabet was invented—or, rather, developed—by the Egyptians, in four stages, from hieroglyphics. Hieroglyphics are picture-writing. All phonetic alphabets have their beginning in hieroglyphic writing. The work of developing a phonetic alphabet from hieroglyphics occupied the Egyptians at least four thousand years. They would, perhaps, have satisfactorily completed the task, but that the use of hieroglyphics, ideograms, and phonograms had such a hold of their conservative minds that they never rose to the untrammeled use of a phonetic alphabet. Belief in the sacredness of the old forms also had its effect in checking their progress. They used the phonetic alphabet, indeed, but so cumbrously that they derived little benefit from its employment. The Egyptian alphabet was taken from Egypt by two or three branches of the great Semitic race. The Phœnicians, the maritime branch of the fam-

ily, did most toward the development of the
alphabet. Of the twenty-four letters in the
Greek alphabet, sixteen are commonly attrib-
uted to the Phœnician Cadmus.

The object and use of an alphabet are to
express in speech every sound that is uttered
by the voice, and, ultimately, in the far higher
development of words, every thought that has
its birth in the mind of man. Five leading
ancient authors assert that the alphabet passed
from Phœnicia into Greece. The best authori-
ties agree in asserting that the Egyptians invented the alphabet, that the Phœnicians
improved it, and that the mental flower of the
Aryan race, the Greeks, in the dawn of their
history, did most to bring it to the stage of
comparative perfection. From *alpha* and *beta*,
the first two letters of the Greek alphabet, in
its ultimate form, the word *alphabet* is derived,
although, by going back further, we find *aleph*
and *beth*, the two corresponding characters in
the Phœnician, or Semitic, alphabet. The first
means an ox, and the second a house. All existing European alphabets have been derived
from that of Phœnicia. To the Greeks great
credit is due for extending the use and signifi-
cation of the vowel sounds. All of the Semitic
alphabets were consonantal; that is, the conso-

nants were the radical elements, and the vowels relational only. The Greeks, in the development of the alphabet they received from the Phœnicians, altered this, exhibiting the mental ability and creative genius they subsequently did in architecture, sculpture, oratory, poetry, and science. They made the vowels the pillars upon which the sound structure, rests. Consonants in their and our alphabets are largely dumb (soundless) without the vowels. For instance, the letters *d - l - l* are soundless; but with the aid of the vowel *e*, they blossom into sound, and become *dell*, significant of flowers, grass, and running water.

In asserting that the invention of the alphabet was, in some respects, the greatest invention of the human mind, probably many will connect the invention with material rather than mental work. The essence of alphabets and words is material, too. That which is most metaphysical, mysterious, and spiritual in both can always be traced back to some physical fact in nature. All picture-writing was drawn from that source, although the analogies were still mental. A picture of a bird (to represent flight), and of the sun (to represent light, brightness, heat, or time), and of a house with a door open (to impart the information that the inhabitant had gone on a journey from the house two suns or days before), was both a material and mental picture; the conveyance of a message as truly to the mind, as far as it went, as the writing of a letter. This is a lower stage of language; and, as I have said, that is where the Egyptians and all other nations began — the majority progressed no further. But beyond this first, this hieroglyphic and ideographic stage, the Egyptians passed to the glory of the true alphabet, their letters being still copied from living animals, or from the sun, moon, or stars, from fields or from trees, but now representing sounds only. The letters have since been so changed that it is very difficult to trace the physical resemblances, although Dr. Isaac Taylor, in his work on the alphabet, has done so with a fair degree of success. In a lecture on this subject, Max Müller said:

"We still write English in hieroglyphics: and, in spite of all the vicissitudes through which the ancient hieroglyphics have passed, in their journey from Egypt to Phœnicia, from Phœnicia to Greece, from Greece to Italy, and from Italy to England, when we write a capital _F_; when we draw the top line and the smaller line through the middle of the letter, we simply draw the two horns of the cerastes, the horned serpent which the ancient Egyptians used for representing the sound of _F_. In the same manner, in writing, the form of our capital _L_ still

recalls very strikingly the bent back of a crouching lion,
which, in the later hieroglyphic inscriptions represents
the sound of *L*."

Dr. Taylor and Max Müller derived all, or
nearly all, their information on this subject
from the learned French Egyptologist, De
Rougé (*Mémoire sur l'Origine Egyptienne de
l'Alphabet Phœnicien: par E. de Rougé, Paris,
1874*). In the transition from the singleness'
and simplicity of the letters of the alphabet
to the combination of words and ideas, resi-
dent in and capable of expression by them,
ages elapsed. The letters, in one sense, were
the raw material only — words, the finished
product; and it is perhaps approximately cor-
rect to say that the distance between letters
and words is as great as between iron in bars
and iron in the works of a watch or in the
steam-engine. The difference between words
as they now exist in English orthography and
as both appeared in the comparatively recent
age of Henry the Eighth is very great. Four
hundred years ago each writer did that which
was right in his own eyes in spelling; but
orthography, through subsequent literary culture, is now bounded by rules nearly as pre-
cise as those of grammar. The alphabet is
the vehicle for the expression of the varying

sounds of the human tongue; words express
the feelings and thoughts — the most tender
or passionate feelings and the most sublime
and instructive thoughts — of the mental and
spiritual powers. They have been truthfully
called the wings of thought. Whether it is
true or false that we cannot even think without words, it is certain that we cannot com-
municate with each other without them.
"Things," Dr. Lewand says, "are thinks"; and
" thinks," Max Müller adds, " are words."

Language, more than anything else, enables
each generation to transmit to its successor,
not alone all its strictly literary treasures
of wisdom and knowledge, but also all its
mechanical, agricultural, metallurgical, and
scientific knowledge. The pecuniary and all
other material wealth transmitted by each
generation to its successor, is of small value
compared to that transmitted by language,
through word of mouth and the printed page.
Speech is friendly, because it cannot be exercised at all without the social state.

Mysterious, wonderful, and elevated as the
alphabet is, it is still only the alphabet, beside
the far higher mental table-land of words.
Our words are, indeed, ourselves. Words best
show a man. " Speak, that I may see thee,"

says Ben Jonson; and again, our Lord, speaking on the most solemn subject to which human attention can be called, that of the final judgment, says: "For by *thy words* thou shalt be justified, and by *thy words* thou shalt be condemned." Our words being ourselves, by them we must stand or fall. Right acts are necessarily accompanied by right words. There is, of course, the strongest possible motive to those engaged in wrong acts to cover or excuse them by right words; but words thus used lose their force, and are seldom able to convince, when the heart and truth are not in them. Deception by looks is easier than deception by words. If we will exercise our memories to remember why we have liked one person and disliked another, we will find that the foundation of our decision was based more upon their speech than upon anything else. Words were given us, a charlatan statesman said, to enable us to conceal our thoughts. This is a lie against nature and against language. And no one, not even the most consummate Machiavelli, who under the guise of a saint is endeavoring to play the devil, can long succeed by his words in deceiving any one. One of the best proofs of this is that ethology means the science of character and a

treatise on morality. Leaving aside the moral
guilt and debasement of the speaker, therefore, altogether, speech itself is debased when
not used on the straight lines of truth.

It is most significant that high deeds in-
volve high language, and low deeds must have
their expression in low language. Sophocles
said to his countrymen, who complained that
he had debased their language: " You do the
deeds, and your ungodly deeds find me the
words." Marsh says: " The men who crawled
to such a tyrant as Tiberius used as lofty language as was used by the fathers of the Roman Republic." It will seem like presumption
to contradict such an authority, but there can
be no doubt that the Roman speech and independence were both alike degraded, by the
body-and-mind-crushing despotism of the five
monsters who were misnamed Cæsars. Of one
period in the reign of Tiberius, Tacitus says :

" At no time was the city in a state of deeper anxiety
and alarm. Men were afraid to meet, afraid to discourse ;
silence and distrust extended alike to strangers and ac-
quaintances, and both were equally divided ; even things
dumb and inanimate, roofs and walls, were regarded
with apprehension. Such was the pestilential character
of those times, so contaminated with adulation, that not
only the first nobles, but all who had been consuls, strove
for priority in the fulsomeness and extravagance of their
votes. . . . 'How fitted for slaves are these men !'

Tiberius constantly said, as he left the Senate. Even *he*
nauseated the crouching tameness of his slaves."

That I am not doing Marsh and his great
works on language injustice, these extracts will
show. Besides, he elsewhere asserts, what is
recognized as a universal truth by all writers
on philology, that the degradation of a nation
means the degradation of its language. Never
was Rome so degraded, not even under her
other imperial monsters (Caligula, Nero, Do-
mitian, or Commodus), as under Tiberius, and
his real ruler, Sejanus. Language as well as
liberty, therefore, undoubtedly suffered. Indeed, one of the most painful things to contemplate in connection with the bondage of a
nation is that its language and literature suffer
no less than the bodies and minds of its people.
The north of England stubbornly resisted
William the Conqueror. He retaliated fearfully, and in beating the people into submis-
sion, he thereby nearly obliterated northern
English culture. Macaulay says that for one
hundred and fifty years after the Norman Conquest there was, to speak strictly, no English
history. The rise of a national literature in
Hungary has twice been crushed by Austrian
oppression; first in the sixteenth and the
second time in this century. Egypt never re-

covered from her crushing conquest by Cambyses. Rome conquered Carthage, and Carthage has left us no literature. On this subject Professor W. D. Whitney, in his work on "Language and the Study of Language," says:

"Phœnicia has left us no literature. The coffin of one of the kings of Sidon, found but a few years since, presents in its detailed inscriptions a fuller view of the Phœnician tongue than is derivable from all its other known records, taken altogether. A few inscriptions and a mutilated and obscure fragment of the Roman poet Plautus, referring to Carthage, are the only relics left us of the idiom of that queenly city."

A Latin translation was made of Mago's work on agriculture, by order of the Roman Senate. When it is remembered that Hamilcar and Hannibal, in all the varied qualities that go to make up great commanders, were unquestionably two of the greatest soldiers of the world, it is forever to be regretted that Rome's triumph left Carthage no less without mental than military existence. Had Carthage triumphed, the case would have been very different. Even the gods worshiped by a conquering people were frequently forced on the conquered. In the Hibbert Lectures, by Sayce, he says that if Bel-Merodach, the chief of the Babylonian pantheon, was lord of other gods, he was so only because the king of Babylon was lord also of other cities and lands. But when Babylonia ceased to be an independent power, the star of supremacy of its chief god also set.

Rome's turn came after that of Carthage: the imperial city was ground down by its tyrants. Its literature, considering that it was mistress of the world for hundreds of years, is pitifully poor, compared to that of Greece. But the genius of the Roman people was not originally directed toward literature, but toward civic virtue, civic obedience, and continued conquest. These are the reasons why Rome never produced any world-work in literature. When conquest left Rome time for mental culture, tyranny, luxury, and vice had smothered freedom, and the faith and truth which had characterized the primitive Roman. Even the two most happily circumstanced and most popular of Roman poets, Virgil and Horace, were mentally shackled. The fact that the hand was gloved, and that the tyrant threw continual flowers and favors in their paths, did not take the gyves off their minds. They were there to puff and praise Augustus chiefly. After the second Punic War, lingual and national decadence began at Rome. All literature was based on Greek models. The Roman mind was almost wholly imitative, and constantly looked back to Greece. Cicero wrote thus to his brother: "I am not ashamed to confess that all my own attainments are due to those studies and those accomplishments which have been handed down to us in the literary treasures and the philosophical system of the Greeks." Rome conquered the world, and her language was long as imperial as her legions and emperors — one eminently of force and command. Rome impressed her language on nearly all of her conquered subjects. She wholly failed to do this with Greece, just as the Mantchus as notably failed with the Chinese, and the Northmen with the French, because the nations conquered in these cases were mentally the superior people. Despite these exceptional facts, however, neither the Greek language under the Romans, the Chinese under the Mantchus, nor the French language in the portion of France ruled by the Normans, was what each would have been had no conquest been achieved over the native people. The Dutch resisted Spanish oppression, and overthrew the then greatest nation of Europe. The result is that the Dutch is a living and separate language in Europe to-day; a philological game bantam, as it were, holding up its head and crowing.

Of Arabic, Dr. Isaac Taylor says: "Of all existing alphabets, the Arabic, both from its literary importance and its geographical extent, ranks next after the great Latin alphabet itself." This is saying very much — for all European alphabets came from the Latin alphabet. Dr. Taylor further says:

"The alphabet of the Koran is now the chief commercial alphabet of the East; it constitutes the official script by means of which three Asiatic empires are ruled, and has been adapted to express the peculiar sounds of languages of the most varied type — Arabic, Turkic, Persian, Pushti, Beluchi, Hindostani, and Malay. That the local alphabet of Mecca should have exterminated all other Semitic scripts and have established itself as the dominant alphabet of Africa and Asia, is an illustration more striking than any other that can be adduced of the power of religious influences in effecting a wide and rapid diffusion of alphabets."

Dr. Taylor in these remarks possibly overlooks the fact that it is doubtful whether Mohammed himself was able to read or write. He also overlooks the real power in this case, which was that of the sword. That has been a more potent influence than any other power in propagating language. In Mohammed's time, prayer took the form of military exercises. Brother would have slain brother, had the Prophet willed it. Conquest came through Mohammed and his successors by the sword first and for Arabic afterwards. "It was in the mosque, where the use of the sword was deified, that the Moslems acquired the *esprit de corps* and that rigid discipline which distinguished their armies." "Aggressiveness," Prof. Wellhausen says, "was in the blood of Mohammed and his followers and successors." "There is no question," says the same authority, "that the material success of Islam was the chief force that attracted new adherents. The unique sovereignty of Allah was induced by the fact that no might could withstand his. In spreading, by means of the sword, the worship of Allah, rich booty was gained."

Practically, Arabic had little or no literature until the sword forced nation after nation under its influence. The Arabs were greatly elevated by becoming the pupils of the nations they conquered. Every man able to bear arms was bound to render military service. The respect, admiration, and awe which mankind has always yielded to military conquerors have a deeper foundation and a higher reason than appears on the surface. To be conquered physically largely means to be conquered mentally, in soul as well as in body.

If a conquered people are elevated intellectually above their victors, they are thereby enabled to some extent to parry the effects of their degradation. The mind and the pen have ultimately in all ages been mightier than the sword. But this elevation and superiority always preceded and never followed conquest; at least until the conquered people had long subsequently achieved independence. The Mantchus, who conquered the Chinese, were a people of no mental culture whatever, while the Chinese are, after the Brahminic Hindoos, the most cultured nation of Asia. China, indeed, it is claimed, is one vast library. The imperial catalogue of national literature forms one hundred and twelve octavo volumes of three hundred pages each. Macaulay speaks of the immortality of the Strulbrugs as representing Chinese civilization; but in this he was greatly mistaken. The Abbé Huc, the best authority on China, says: "From about 1644, China went through fifteen changes of dynasties, all accomplished by bloody revolutions and civil wars. This means anything but political or mental stagnation. Repeatedly subjected to foreign domination, China has always vanquished her conquerors, compelling them implicitly to adopt her civilization and

respect and maintain her institutions." She
was still, however, degraded by conquest. The
shaving of the head and wearing of the pig-
tail are evidences of servitude imposed by her
present masters.

The Chinese have no true alphabet. They
have two hundred and thirty-four key characters, each of which is a monosyllable. There
are about one hundred thousand words in their
vocabulary. This large stock of words, in an
uninflected language, is formed by joining
syllable to syllable. Instead of saying *parents*,
they say *father-mother*. The word *average* is
expressed by *not-greatness, not-smallness; brother-
brother* is *oldest brother; lady-lady* is *great lady*.
A man may trade with unequaled success
on a small capital of words in Chinese. Sir
George Stanton says the Chinese penal stat-
utes are all written in eight hundred words.
This is remarkable when it is remembered
that in China all laws are penal.

The language of a nation, more than anything else, shows the genius of the people. No
nation of the earth has accomplished so much
in the arts, mechanics, and agriculture with
such small material as the Chinese. This is
especially true of them in the art of arts,
agriculture, and is still more true of what they

have accomplished in language. Their language is yet in the rudeness of infancy — the isolating stage, — and yet no nation of the earth, perhaps, can point to a more extensive literature. Its quality, too, is worthy of admiration, judged even by the highest civilized standard.

The triumphs of a nation, either in the military, literary, scientific, or mechanical sense, mean triumphs for its language and literature. But where there has always been mental stagnation and physical isolation, as in the case of the Tartars, a people may overrun and destroy surrounding nations and yet themselves remain in barbarism. Genghis Khan left to his successors, an empire which extended from the China Sea to the Dnieper, and yet he impressed nothing whatever on the nations he conquered but the remembrance of his horrible massacres. After Tartar conquest and massacres, it was said that " no eye remained open to weep for the dead." Note, however, that the word *Mongol* is from the root *mong*, which means brave. They had bravery, and that only.

English soldiers have been conquerors everywhere, and, behind wooden walls, English seamen won immortal victories; while her navigators discovered almost innumerable islands, and what is believed to be an Antarctic continent. The ships of her merchants and mercantile adventurers have fretted all seas. The English language would not now be what it is — mentally and philologically the most perfect and most conquering language of the earth — but for these facts. Yet there was a time, lasting for about three hundred years after the Norman conquest, when the Anglo-Saxon language was in the utmost danger of obliteration. It is asserted by Macaulay that it would have perished but for the separation from France, through fortunate failure to conquer that country.

Queen Mary said that if her heart was examined after death Calais would be found written on it, so deeply did its loss affect her. But its loss, and that of all France to English arms, was a vital gain to English language and literature. After the Norman conquest, the Saxon language and literature went into bondage with the Saxon people. Saxon and Norman words fought as fiercely for supremacy as Norman and Saxon men. When, finally, the two people began to coalesce on terms of equality, and to become brother Englishmen, the language showed — nay, still shows, — native losses then suffered. Halliwell's dictionary of archaic and provincial words contains over fifty thousand words not recorded in modern dictionaries. Saxon grammar remained comparatively intact — for grammar, called the blood and soul of language, is nearly indestructible; but Saxon words and Saxon inflections both suffered, and that in their best elements, too, — the language of poetry and of the affections, of the marketplace and of the home. Unquestionably, our English vocabulary is far richer and more copious, especially in the technical terms used in astronomy, botany, mineralogy, chemistry, etc., for the additions it received from the Normans. French words were first blended with Anglo-Saxon by the genius of Chaucer and Spenser; but the additions were so abundant, so overflowing in number, and in many cases so superfluous, that those made then and since were not so much additions as the adding of a new language to English, an addition that prevented the growth of Anglo-Saxon and remitted to obscurity many words the loss of which is ever to be regretted, and can never wholly be atoned. There is one comforting fact, however; words of French origin, often unregretted, drop out of use and are never restored to verbal circulation again; whereas, if a homely but earnest Anglo-Saxon word drops out of use, its loss is regretted, and it is frequently restored and always welcomed back.

The highest, the most spiritual, the most mysterious thing about man is his speech. It is a remarkable fact that nothing can be added to or subtracted from the body of any language. The language may be nearly obliterated by conquest, as was the Ancient Celtic and others herein named, but it cannot be changed. Every language, no matter how barbarous, is complete in itself. No such thing is known as a language in transition. Forms change; even the roots of a language may be disguised, but they cannot possibly be altered —their essential element, their fundamental meaning, survives all change. Roots predicative and roots demonstrative remain, as Max Müller asserts, as the ultimate analysis of all language. The Hindoos were the first to trace all words back to roots. Prof. Max Müller claims that all of the words, numbering at least two hundred and fifty thousand, in the English dictionary, whether of native or imported speech, the near and far alike, can be traced back to eight hundred roots, and these to one hundred and twenty-one fundamental

ideas or concepts. From this latter original
stock have been forged words and meaning
enough to give expression to every thought
that ever passed through the mind of man.
Never before did man erect so divine a temple
from such apparently insignificant materials.
Never did he appear so godlike as in thus
forging the thunderbolts of speech. Here,
if ever, he wielded the powers of Jupiter
Tonans.

It is a remarkable fact, and one tending
to the glory of mental democracy, that the
great works of the imagination and of poetry
were produced by men nearly innocent of
schools and scholarship. Homer, Shakespeare,
Cervantes, De Foe, Bunyan, Goldsmith, Burns,
and Abraham Lincoln were all self-taught
men, and nearly all spoke one language only.
So, too, measured by our almost immeasurably
extended standard, were Æschylus, Sophocles,
Euripides, and Aristophanes. If Milton had
not been a schoolman, he would probably have
been an immeasurably greater, because an un-
conscious, poet. This fact he himself recognized. Macaulay doubted that we should have
had Lear if Shakespeare had been able to read
Sophocles in Greek. The very best and most
earnest words in the four great languages of

the world — Greek, Latin, German, and English — came from the common people. The language of Luther, of the English Bible, and of Shakespeare, was in each case a language that the unlearned used and could understand. The best words of the Attic dialect, the *lingua Romana,* and the mother tongue in Anglo-Saxon, were all not only coined, but long circulated first amongst the common people. The French Academy, composed of the mental and scientific rulers of France, never gave a word to the French language; street gamins and peasants are constantly adding to it; they first stamp the words as being of sterling philological value, and the learned finally, and often most unwillingly, come to their use. When a language became a dead one, it was always killed by the over-culture of the learned, as the dressing of wheat in milling deprives it of the material from which bone and muscle—the pillars of the human body—are erected. The best and most forcible, the most earnest, and most truthful language is democratic rather than aristocratic. Dante was a scholar, and his immortal work may seem to contradict these statements; but in his Divine Comedy he used, though, of course, he sometimes refined, the dialect of peasants and market-women.

Macaulay's tribute to Dante was, perhaps, the highest ever paid to a latter-day author: "Dante," he says, "used the fewest and best words it is possible to use."

The highest and best meaning of words is not found in dictionaries, where the words are disconnected, but in the best authors, who, by the exercise of one of the highest gifts of genius, place words in such living and happy combinations that, married in sentences, they produce mental pictures from which are derived at once the greatest mental profit and the highest mental pleasure. A word standing alone is but the link of a chain; its greatest strength and highest use can be attained only by combination. Genius only can in such cases link and combine words to produce the happiest and best results of meaning. On this subject Marsh says: "Dictionary definitions, considered as a means of philological instruction, are as inferior to miscellaneous reading as a herbarium to a botanic garden. The vocabulary of the passions and the affections lives and breathes only in mutual combinations." In the selection of the very best words to express in poetry the warmest feelings of the heart and highest mental powers, Chaucer rendered higher service than any other Eng-

lishman. And yet, if he had been more of the
people and less of the court, there would have
been much more Anglo-Saxon in English than
there now is; the language, indeed, would
have been almost radically different. No one
affects a language like a great poet. God and
great poets, say the Italians, are the only
creators. Shakespeare and the translators of
the Bible were greatly indebted to Chaucer.
Marsh calls him "the Charlemagne of the
new intellectual dynasty of England. He
unites what was best in Latin and Anglo-Saxon
words, and produced a polyglottic vocabulary
which is superior to that of either language
separately." In this connection, note how the
Bible is *the Book*, in another than the Chris-
tian sense. Macaulay says of it: "At the time
when that odious style which deforms the
writings of Hall and Lord Bacon was almost
universal, appeared that stupendous work, the
English Bible, a book which, if everything
else in our language should perish, would alone
suffice to show the whole extent of its beauty
and power." It has been frequently said that
the translators of the Bible were inspired.
Our greatest translation, that of the time of
King James, was made in the language of the
common people. If the claim of inspiration

rested only upon that fact, which, of course, it does not, then the Latin proverb, " *Vox populi, vox Dei*," ("The voice of the people is the voice of God,") would be true in a higher sense than that in which it has been generally understood. And there are high and valid philological reasons why this is so. The language of the common people is closest to nature — material nature,— in which, it cannot be too firmly remembered, the foundations on which *all* that is best, most vital, and truthful in all languages are laid. Therefore, he who used the people's language used the highest, because the most natural, simple, and powerful language with which man's attention can be aroused, his reason convinced, his affections and mental and spiritual powers led captive. Nature here means — as she, indeed, always does mean — earnestness, truth, simplicity, beauty and power.

One of the most noticeable, and yet one of the most natural, facts about such a mental man of men as Shakespeare, is that no author, poet, or dramatist has ever imitated, or even tried to imitate, his style. The attempt has not been made, and if made, could not hope to attain even that success which the maker of artificial fruit and flowers achieves. In making them, form and color may at least be mechanically imitated; but *none* of Shakespeare's greatest qualities are imitable. In this respect he is alone, with all of the authors of the world surrounding him. Shakespeare's language, simple though its general characteristic is, is one of the most wonderful features that stamp him as " not for a day, but for all time."

One of the strongest illustrations of how people can be degraded in a moral and philological sense, while they were ardently devoted to literary and artistic progress, is afforded by the Italian Renaissance. Sculpture, architecture, painting, poetry, and general literature never won more astonishing triumphs than in that era — not even in the Golden Age of Greece. Petrarch was crowned with greater honors than are accorded to a military conqueror. Michel Angelo was an autocrat who dictated terms to a tyrannical Pope. Lorenzo de Medici was called the Magnificent, far more for his mental ability and culture, his patronage of art and learning, and his devotion to the discovery of ancient manuscripts illustrating classical learning, than for his enormous wealth, his remarkable abilities as a ruler, and his lovableness as a man.

But while Italy was thus exalted in a literary and artistic sense, it was never more degraded morally. Such personages as the Borgias, Pazzis, and Machiavellis were guilty of murder by poisoning and other forms of assassination, and of adultery and incest, or else defended these crimes. They lied and deceived with a countenance indicative of the utmost candor, and with a boldness that would have deceived the closest reader of faces and actions. These were the leaders in art and literature, no less than the rulers in the government and social life. In the debasement which they created, language suffered in a vital, because a moral, sense.

A wretch, an assassin who stabbed swiftly, unexpectedly, and devilishly, was a *bravo*, a brave man,— and he *was* brave, compared to those who hired him. A devotee of music, art, or of learning, was, and is yet, a *virtuoso*, devoted to the virtues, although his private life may have been black and despicable. A prostitute or mistress had her sin removed, in the social and legal sense at least, in the knowledge that society attached no stigma either to her name or conduct. A bastard inherited equally with legitimate children. The Italian language yet bears strong traces of this moral debasement and of the crushing despotism to which the people's liberties were then and have until lately been subjected. Grandiloquent terms are used for the most trifling articles, and an obsequiousness of thanks akin to crawling is returned for the most trifling favors. Leigh Hunt gives many painful philological illustrations of these facts. Such exaggeration and obsequiousness of language has in it no sincerity, no heart, and is born at once of the degraded condition of those who use it and of their poverty. The Russians of to-day are a nation of shameless liars, because they are cowed by despotism. Lying and debasement of language in such cases are not to be so harshly judged as in a land of mental light and liberty. Lying is a refuge of the weak and oppressed — " the vice of slaves," as it is termed by Plutarch.

Language always conforms to the institutions of the country in which it is spoken. Asiatic lands furnish the strongest illustration of this principle. The dull, oppressed native Hindoo, not figuratively or partially, but actually and wholly, crawled before his superior, in a monetary or social sense; and his language partook of and reflected his degradation. The punishment prescribed in the Hindoo Vedas for a Sudra who attempted either to hear a priest recite or to raise himself in any way above his utterly sunken condition was to the last degree cruel and arbitrary. The Sudras are the farmers and workers of India. They composed three-fourths of the natives of that country. As a consequence, their language is as much a pariah and a product of poverty of mind and spirit, and of utter degradation, ignorance, and poverty, as they themselves. The Gypsy language and grammar equally illustrate the effect of ages of roaming vagrancy and illiteracy.

The nation that enjoys an upright, self-asserting, self-respecting use of words must have successfully demonstrated its courage before domestic and foreign tyrants, and be in the van of national progress and of mental light and physical liberty. If it loses the latter, it must to some extent lose its language, in the highest and best sense. The decline of Rome, in the sense of a fall of its liberties, is generally dated from the time of Marius, Sulla, Pompey, Crassus, and Julius Cæsar. But that fall really began after the second Punic War; and it is an historical fact, related by Polybius, that the Roman of his day could not read the treaties between Rome and Carthage, so great had been the changes in Latin. The language, like the people, had lost the ancient earnestness, truth, and simplicity. It had gained in copiousness of vocabulary; but this gain was paid for by loss of simplicity and virility, in the moral and social sense. The Apostle Paul charged certain professors with having a form of godliness, but denying the power thereof. Language, in like manner, may retain the form, the words, while the truth, life, earnestness, and simplicity — the soul, in short,— has departed. It may have a name to live, while it is radically dead.

The reign of Louis the Fourteenth has been called, and very justly, the Augustan age of French literature. Authors in both those ages were subsidized to write or sing the glories of despots. But literature and art, shackled by royal bounties and the prostitution born of them, were largely marked by toadyism and the loss of life thereby created. The king named was treated always as a deity. Those who have seen the paintings still remaining on the walls of Versailles know this. The king once removed an official, who, wishing to regain royal favor, addressed the words of the fifty-first Psalm to him, " Cast me not away from Thy presence, and take not Thy Holy Spirit from me." On this subject, Buckle says:

" The French, in spite of the heroic efforts of the Fronde, not only fell under the despotism of Louis the Fourteenth, but never even cared to resist it, and at length, becoming slaves in their souls as well as in their bodies, they grew proud of a condition which the meanest Englishman would have spurned as an intolerable bondage. As if to exhaust every form of absurdity, the most serious misunderstanding arose as to who should have the honor of giving the king his napkin as he sat at meals, and who was to enjoy the inestimable privilege of helping the queen on with her shift. It should be remembered that these occurrences, and above all the importance formerly attached to them, is part of the history of the French mind. The end of this was a corruption, a servility, and a loss of power more complete than has ever been witnessed in any of the great countries of Europe."

Words can have their dignity wantonly insulted and lowered by intentional misuse. *Lex*, as is well known, means *law* in Latin, and *Rex, king*. Some one, Laud or Strafford, aiding Charles the First in his attempt to make himself superior to law, said that he had often heard that *rex* was *lex*, but that he never before heard that *lex* was *rex*. This doctrine was derived from James the First, who laid down the despotic maxim, *A Dio rex, a rege lex.* War was fought to settle the meaning of the two words first named. The result showed all law-breakers, king as well as subject, that law was king of kings in England. The English language no less than English liberty was vitally interested in this contest. Note, on the other hand, the utter degradation of a country where the king was not only the law temporal but spiritual. Of Philip the Second, a contemporary, struck by the universal homage he received, said: "The Spanish people do not merely love, merely reverence, but absolutely adore him, and deem his commands so sacred that they could not be violated without offense to God." Loyalty and superstition went hand in hand in Spain; ignorance ruled, and language was necessarily degraded.

The English aristocracy was greatly degraded in the reign of the heartless, corrupt, immoral, and wholly unpatriotic Charles the Second. Lords and other aristocrats acted as waiters on their knees, in serving the king at table. French manners and customs were slavishly followed by king and courtiers. Literature was very much debased also, but this debasement did not extend to the common people; and, therefore, language did not suffer materially, nor national progress either, in a legislative sense at least,— for some of the best laws preservative of the freedom of the people and press were passed in that reign. What was true of public men and

literature in the time of Charles remained
more or less true during all the succeed-
ing reigns, until late in George the Third's
time. If the works of a majority of authors
of the time of Charles the Second, James, and
William and Mary could be blotted out, language would suffer little loss, while clean
literature would be a decided gainer. This
is particularly true of dramatic works and
poetry, so-called.

We are accustomed to think of George the
Third as having been a tyrant, only or mostly
in his treatment of the American colonies,
which he first exasperated into rebellion,
and thereby finally ennobled into independence; but, in his home policy, he really
struck at English liberty and the English
language even more fatally, had he succeeded
in striking successfully. In 1771, writing to
Lord North on the subject of publishing par-
liamentary debates (the people being desirous
of knowing what their law-makers were doing), he said: "It is highly necessary that this
strange and careless method of publishing
debates should be put a stop to. But is not
the House of Lords the best court to bring
such miscreants before; as it can fine as well
as imprison, and has broader shoulders to

support the odium of so salutary a measure?"
Now, had this weak and tyrannical king succeeded in suppressing the publication of par-
liamentary reports, the word *miscreant* would
have acquired two new meanings. From the
king's and his abettors' side it would have
meant those who were guilty of the crime, in
their eyes, of wanting to know what Parliament
was doing, while from the people's side it would
have meant those who were opposed to tyranny.
Buckle says: "Every liberal sentiment, everything approaching to reform — nay, even the
mere mention of inquiry,— was abomination in
the eyes of that narrow and ignorant prince."
The right to prevent meetings was lodged in
an irresponsible appointee of the crown. If a
meeting of even twelve persons persisted in
discussing public questions for an hour after
a magistrate ordered them to disperse, the
penalty was death. It is alleged that the
word *independence*, in its modern acceptation,
does not occur in our language before the
early part of the eighteenth century. Ser-
vile imitation of the French was the fashion
during a large part of the long period named,
and words of Latin or French origin were
very much used. Professor Morley says of
De Foe: "He also reformed the currency of

English speech, which in his time had been lowered by French alloy." Literary feebleness was then long married to immorality. Tawdry images were much used in the description of natural objects. Nearly everything was unnatural, soulless, and insincere — utterly foreign to the genius and spirit of what is best in English language and literature.

It is well known that all European languages are derived from the Aryan speech, which came from the highlands of Asia. Professor Sayce attempted to prove that this speech came from the north of Europe; but he himself has abandoned that theory, I believe. The word *Aryan* is from the root *ar*, one of whose fundamental meanings is *to plow*. A plowing, an agricultural people were superior to those who lived by pastoral pursuits or by hunting.

In its wealth of words, modern English is one of the most composite of languages. The Latin or Norman words, of course, vastly preponderate over other foreign elements in its vocabulary. This element represents probably one-third of the words in the English dictionary; but English-speaking people, having been foremost in exploration, and the greatest in maritime and inland conquest and commercial enterprise, their language has thereby had a larger number of foreign words admitted to its stock of vocables than any other language. It is a striking fact that the intellectual revival in England, from 1485 to 1600, was simultaneous with maritime discovery, military and naval conquests, and mercantile adventure. The foreign words introduced into English then and since have been naturalized into the body of the language, and had the bridle of its grammar imposed upon them; but they are still not of the household. Anglo-Saxon would be much poorer in words relating to the arts, sciences, and jurisprudence if it had not been for a long period dominated by the Norman tongue; but if this mastery had never occurred, it would be richer in words expressive of truth, of the home affections and duties, and of morals and religion. Its richness, for the highest and best poetical uses, would likewise have been greater. Even as it is, however, it is the most richly endowed, in its own still preserved native resources, of any language of the world. That wealth was best illustrated in immeasurably the greatest era of its history, between the beginning of the reign of Henry the Eighth and the close of that of James the First.

Latin and Greek have much greater con-

ciseness of expression than English, because
they are fully inflected languages, while English is most like to Chinese, which is wholly
uninflected. English, too, is constantly becoming more uninflected, brief, and direct. Its
constant tendency is to abolish genders, tenses,
and degrees of comparison. Its collocation and
arrangement of prepositions, nouns, and verbs
are shorter, stronger, clearer, and more unalter-
able in expression than either Latin, Greek or
German. It dispenses with inflections almost
entirely, and relies instead on the collocation
or syntax — that is, on the relative position of
words in sentences. It is in this way that the
English language is unconsciously but certainly
approaching to Chinese, which is the simplest
and most philosophical language in the world.
Max Müller calls Chinese a language *comme
il faut* — that is, a language as it should be.
On this subject, Professor Sayce says: "If the
excellence of a language is to be decided by
the attainment of terseness and vividness,
Chinese would come to the front. English has
fitted itself to become a universal language, by
struggling to assimilate its condition to that
of Chinese." In these facts, which are facts of
brevity, simplicity, and constant tendency to
abolish grammar, lie one of the chief claims

of English to becoming a universal language. Professor Sayce says: "The prophecy has already been hazarded that Pigeon-English, or a similar grammarless jargon, will be the future medium of universal intercourse." If some European language is to be acquired by Oriental and savage people, their language will undoubtedly be English, even if the opportunity offered them to acquire French, Italian, or German were equally good, and the reason for the choice of English would lie in the facts stated. "The English language," says Professor Sayce, "is quite as good an instrument of thought as Sanscrit or Greek, and yet English can hardly be said to be inflectional in the way that Sanscrit and Greek are." If the world is to have a universal language, it will not be, by whatever else it may be characterized, a language of concealment, but one of naked simplicity and directness, both in expression and meaning. Earnestness will also be one of its striking characteristics. If that universal language is to be the English, words of Romance origin will no longer form, as they now do, about fifteen per cent. of the vocabulary used, but will dwindle down to three, four, or five per cent. It may be stated, as a fact indicative of progress in this direction, that, though

words of foreign derivation have vastly increased, in the extension and cultivation of
chemistry, mineralogy, metallurgy, and in the
arts and sciences generally, the number of such
words used in general English literature is now
about twenty-five per cent. less than in the age
of Queen Anne.   In the vocabulary of an ordinary speaker, every word of Anglo-Saxon is
now included.   No disrespect whatever is here
intended either to the Romance languages or to
the people who speak them.   The differences
referred to are explicable by historical facts.
Under ancient Rome, in all its history, people
were ground down.   In its earlier history military duty and conquest, slaughter, and blood
were the great objects in the life of the people
and rulers.   In the later stages these objects
were still most followed and admired, but added
to these was the rule of the Cæsars, which let
loose all the floodgates of evil, in despotism,
vice, effeminate luxury, lying, and deceit. The
language, like the people, became fearfully debased ; men cowered, and in using language
they had to inflate, conceal, and deceive. Later
on, in Italy, France, and Spain, there was, to
say the least, much more in the government,
rulers, and social customs to keep up these
habits than to dissipate them.   In the case of

the Northmen, they were always free. They were, indeed, free-booters and savages, but they became Christianized, civilized, and softened with remarkable rapidity. Note how the Icelanders, at first a most bloodthirsty people, have become one of the most gentle and hospitable races in the world. The scenes witnessed in Paris between 1789 and 1793, and in 1871, could never have occurred in Sweden, Denmark, or Norway. But why? Because those nations never had their bodies, minds, and language crushed for long ages, as have the people of the Latin races.

Of France in the eighteenth century a great writer said: "If ever there existed a state of society likely by its crying and accumulated evils to madden men to desperation, France was in that state. The people, despised and enslaved, were sunk in abject poverty, and were crushed by laws of stringent cruelty, enforced with merciless barbarism." The recoil and revolt were proportionate to the long crushing and degradation. Taine says that, at the time of the Revolution, out of twenty-six million Frenchmen, only one million could read, and in political matters only five hundred or six hundred were competent. What the aristocrats thought of the common people is illus-

trated by the assertion quoted by De Tocque-
ville in his *Ancien Régime*, that Madame du
Chatelet had no objection to undress before
her servants, as she was not convinced that
valets were men. The insolence of language of
the one class, and the cringing humility of
that of the other, can therefore easily be imagined. The effect of suddenly loosing the
shackles of this nation of mental slaves, and
assuring them that they were able to rule
themselves without aid, and that their great
duty was to crush their oppressors and render
it impossible for them ever again to rule, was
like putting human minds into human tigers
and letting them loose to glut their appetites
for blood and revenge.

The Anglo-Saxon is to our tongues, what
father, mother, sister, brother are to our
hearts. Words from other languages have
been admitted into our household, but they
do not live under the same roof-tree. Many
of them are of thin and cold-blooded relation-
ship only. It is a striking fact that, *father,
mother, sister, brother*, are all Anglo-Saxon;
father-in-law, mother-in-law, sister-in-law, uncle
and *aunt*, are either half or wholly of Romance
origin. The best general account of the difference between other languages and Anglo-

Saxon is, that the latter is the mother tongue. And this is one of the strongest claims of the Anglo-Saxon to be the universal language of the future. The Latin, under Rome, was *Patrius Sermo*, the father's speech.

The steamship and the locomotive, by the promotion of commercial intercourse, are two of the strongest possible auxiliaries to assimilation of languages. They are democratic, too, in the sense that they tend to spread, not the language of the learned, but of trade and of the common people. Barbarism and isolation vastly increase, while civilization and intercourse reduce the number of languages. Professor Sayce says: " Destroy literature and facility of inter-communication, and the language of England and America would soon be as different as those of France and Italy." Language, especially of heathen nations, must be elevated before the world can be morally elevated and purified. Missionary labors have shown that the heathen nations cannot be converted until their language has undergone moral re-creation. Where there are no words expressive of purity, morality, truth, honesty, candor, and good faith — where, in fact, spirituality is wanting in a language,— how can the people who speak it be elevated to Christianity or be converted to its pure and high tenets? Here, perhaps, is best seen the truth of the assertion, heretofore made in these pages, that the language is the people.

The Greek authors, especially Aristophanes, did much to lower the moral and spiritual dignity of many words. Words used as trumpets by Æschylus were used as baubles by Aristophanes. The latter's filthy definition of freedom, is perhaps the strongest case in point. How could language fail to be debased and to suffer, when the great men of Athens considered that the objects of life were dominion and lust; that love, self-sacrifice, and devotion were fictions, and that oaths were only good for deception. The Sophists, Dr. Draper says, urged the cultivation of rhetoric, that noble art by which the wrong may be made to appear right and the worse the better cause; by which he who has committed a crime may so mystify society as to delude it into the belief that he is worthy of praise. This is the very depth of philological, and, therefore, of moral, degradation. " Base is the slave that pays," said Falstaff. This is a code of morals to which every Jeremy Diddler would give a cheerful assent, and not suppose, either, that in thus reversing the laws of honesty, he would also be assaulting language. If this rule were adopted, the word *honesty*, in its usual sense, would be in danger of erasure. In numerous islands of the South Pacific that word has never been called into existence; *honesty*, with *virtue, truth, gratitude, love*, and many like words, being utterly unknown. Not to have knowledge of these virtues, and therefore not to have any word expressive of them, is not nearly so bad as first to have them and then, through moral declension, to lose them. Murder was thus almost erased as a crime, when assassination by poisoning was in Italy described as only "assisting" the death of a victim; and in France administering a fatal powder, to expedite the death of one from whom a fortune was expected, was jocularly called "giving a powder of succession." In the fall in the meaning of the word *indolence* a lie was inserted. It declined into the meaning of not to grieve or have pain. But the lie has been ejected, and the word has gone back to its true meaning of laziness, a habit inevitably productive of pain and sorrow, instead of true ease and enjoyment. Trench says: "Far more and mightier in every way is a language than any one of the works which may have been composed in it."

This is true of all but the very greatest works; but the assertion is not true of the Bible or of Shakespeare, at least. In these two works spiritual and mental temples were erected from the stones of language whose summits reach unto heaven; and yet their height is not so wonderful as their wisdom, simplicity, strength, grace, harmony, and beauty. It is, indeed, hardly possible to conceive of any author erecting mental structures more lofty and sublime than those found in these two books, although every word in the vocabulary was used in the effort. Was Italian greater than the use Dante made of it? Can language, while yet in words simply — that is, detached,— ever be so great as when used in combination by inspired prophets, apostles, sages, and poets? It was created for the latter; and in the two books named we have in the one case men inspired of God spiritually, and in the other mentally, creating works the wisdom, beauty, and full meaning of which no man has ever yet been able even to pretend to fathom.

It is generally admitted that no language is more moral and truthful, in the sense of earnestness and directness of meaning, than the English. It will talk earnestly, plainly,

and truthfully; it is a philological hitter,
straight out from the shoulder. Much greater
modesty is displayed in English, too, than in
languages of Latin origin or in Latin itself.
Those who have read Tacitus in Latin and in
English, or the memoirs of St. Simon in
French and English, will understand this.
No modesty or concealment is thought necessary in the majority of Continental languages
of Latin origin. The support which English
has received from the Bible in these directions
has never been, as far as I know, sufficiently
understood or acknowledged. St. Paul and
St. John are known to the world at large only
as apostles of Christ. Few know that, in
addition, they were unsurpassed masters of
language. Never was greater brevity, strength,
power, persuasion, and spiritual and moral
beauty evolved from words than these men
exhibited in their use. No great sculptor,
painter, or poet ever attained his nearest
approach to perfection but by the yielding
of his higher powers and genius to the most
intense earnestness and love of his subject;
and he who wishes to see a writer's soul
thrown into his words must consult the two
inspired writers named. Words in the hands
of such authors — in the hands of *all* really

great authors — become irradiated with divine life, strength, light, and beauty; whereas, when used for deception or in any way to excuse moral turpitude, these elements must go out of them. Their pillars, deflected from the plumb line, begin to totter and to fall. A coniferous tree and a lighthouse have both to withstand strong assaults — the one from wind, and the other from waves. Their strength and ability to overcome these assaults lie in having their center of gravity near their base. The center of gravity of words — their strength, likewise,— is in their roots, their foundations.

In conclusion, it is necessary to remind all readers that the language they use is not their own, but belongs to the race. Untold labor was spent on the best languages — untold sacrifice of blood, suffering, and study, in elevating and preserving them in their present stage of liberty and purity. Language, then, is a sacred heritage, to be used with respect, and with constant aim after truth and simplicity, which always mean power. A solemn duty rests upon all to contribute toward the elevation of language by the use of what is best and highest in words; words that shall not debase, but elevate and refine. The author does not absolutely assert that great authors cannot be rightly appreciated by those who have not studied philology; but he does say that, after such study, they will be much better understood, and afford much greater mental pleasure.

Immortality of the Big Trees.

Immortality of the Big Trees.

THE gigantic height and girth of the *Coniferæ* of California and Oregon have elicited universal wonder and admiration. The botanist who first discovered and described them, and who in his lonely wanderings suffered untold hardships in the search (David Douglass), said that he could not contemplate the redwoods and the Douglass spruce without feelings of the deepest awe. So far as the writer knows, no reasons have ever been given for the great size of these trees. The ice of the glacial period, which drove them from their original homes in the far north, to points much farther south than where they are now found, planed and ground down the solid rock of their present mountain homes. The resulting *detritus*, still existing there in ancient moraines, forms rich forest soil. The force, therefore, which exiled them from their old home at length prepared another. This glacial grinding and apparent degradation resulted in mountain architecture of the most Cyclopean and wonderful character, as revealed in the Yosemites of California and Norway, in which domed-rock structure

predominates. Lifeless, cold, and unpitying
the glacial ice-tools may have been; but they
graved and chiseled in curves, making beauty
wherever they went.

Although the moraine soil aids very rapid
growth in our gigantic conifers, they attain to
massive proportions and their greatest age
without it. One of the very largest sequoias
of the Sierra Nevada was found on a dry hill-
side by Mr. John Muir, the well-known California botanist and geologist. This tree had
a diameter of thirty-five feet eight inches, ex-
clusive of the bark. Mr. Muir estimated its
age, by counting the annual rings, to be over
four thousand years. It had evidently grown
very slowly, because its food was not the
mountain meal of a moraine, but hard fare
obtainable from rock; its chief sustenance,
indeed, was derived from the air: yet very
large growth and comparative immortality
were exhibited by that tree. What, then, were
the other elements to which it was indebted
for its massive size and great age? The answer
is, a constant and full supply of never-frozen
water at the roots, a still greater daily supply
of warm, unclouded sunshine. This continuous, rich, life-giving sunshine is one of the
most remarkable features of the Pacific coast

climate, but especially of the Sierra Nevada.

Whether the oldest sequoias be fifteen hundred or four thousand years old is not the vital point. That point rests on the fact that not a single one of these big trees has yet been found showing any evidence of the feebleness of old age or of natural decay — not one! Fires deface and consume them; storms, when the trees are in exposed situations, may prostrate, and lightning (a frequent agent in their destruction) may blast and destroy, or set fire to them; but natural decay and death have not yet marked or defiled them. The continuity of unclouded light undoubtedly has very much to do with this. On page 42 of "*Bogens Indveindring*," the assertion is made, that the trees requiring most light are content with the poorest soils, and *vice versa*. The almost miraculous rapidity with which crops mature in the brief summers close to or within the Arctic Circle is undoubtedly due, more than is generally imagined, quite as much to the continuity of sunlight as to an extra supply of sun-heat.

Without sunlight, chlorophyl cannot be formed, and without the latter agent carbonic acid and water cannot be decomposed and assimilated in plants. How much heat is produced by the absorption of light by the leaves of the big *Coniferæ*, or by deciduous trees, can not yet be told; but, no doubt, the amount has a very sensible effect in stimulating the growth and sustenance of the trees. Clear sunshine is continuous in the Sierra Nevada of California from about June to November; and even in the so-called winter months there are, on the average, five days of clear weather overhead to two of clouds and rain or falling snow, even when the snow is on the ground to a depth of from five to forty feet. I have repeatedly been in the upper Sierra Nevada on snowshoes, in winter, when the weather overhead was as clear as in June, and when the thermometer one hundred feet above the snow covering must have registered from seventy to eighty degrees in the sun. February in the valleys of California answers to the June of the Atlantic States as a growing month.

All of the great *Coniferæ*, but especially the big sequoias, have a heavy and widespreading mass of sponge-like roots, which arrest and hold sufficient moisture for constant irrigation. There is, indeed, such a superabundance of water, that springs are constantly found issuing from the base of these trees. Now, the growth of trees is as much stimulated by irrigation as that of food plants. By constructing lateral irrigating ditches on hillsides in Europe, firs grew to twice the size of those found in dry soil adjoining. In other experiments, irrigated trees grew seven times as fast as those not having the advantage of artificial watering. The sequoias, therefore, are under the most constant stimulus of elements most vital at once to their health and growth. The water around their roots, too, is never frozen. When occasional severe frosts prevail, and the thermometer, under their stress, descends to its greatest depth (about five degrees below zero), the ground is covered by snow, which maintains the warmth of both roots and soil. This is not the least of the causes tending to the continuous growth, massive size, health, and therefore great age, of the big trees of California. The *Coniferæ* of New England cease growing in the late summer and fall; they then begin to store up vitality to withstand the cold of winter, as hibernating animals do.

Although the growth of the great *Coniferæ* of California is continuous, there is no overstimulation in it. The growth is so perfectly natural, and so eminently healthy and strong, that it comes nearer resulting in immortal life in these trees than the age exhibited by any other trees or any other living thing in the world. Some other trees enumerated by the late Dr. Asa Gray have also records of very great age.

" Trees [he says] far outlast all other living things, and form familiar and appropriate symbols of long protracted existence. . . . We are therefore naturally led to inquire, whether there is any absolute limit to their existence. If not destroyed by accident—that is, by extrinsic cause of whatever sort,—do trees, like ourselves, eventually perish from old age? The unavoidable induration and incrustation of its cells and vessels, apart from other causes, would put an early and sure limit to the life of the tree, just as it does, in fact, terminate the existence of the leaf, the proper emblem of mortality, which, although it generally only lives a single season, may be said to truly die of old age. . . . The old and central part of the trunk may, indeed, decay; but this is of little moment, so long as new layers are regularly formed at the circumference. The tree survives, and it is difficult to show that it is liable to death from old age, in any proper sense of the term. . . . Though the wood in the center of the trunks and larger branches, the product of leaves and buds that have long ago disappeared, may die and decay, yet, while new individuals are formed on the surface with each successive crop of fresh buds, and placed in as favorable communication with the soil and air as their predecessors, the aggregate tree would appear to have no necessary, no inherent limit to its existence. . . . This doctrine of the indefinite longevity of trees —that they die from injury or disease, or, in one word, from accidents, but never from old age,—was first propounded by the distinguished De Candolle, near the commencement of the present century."

All of the remarkably aged specimens of various species in all portions of the world enumerated by Dr. Gray show some signs of decrepitude or decay. Death was at work somewhere in their center or circumference. I am not able to assert that the sequoias are the *only* exception, but they certainly are *an* exception, to this rule. If they have any companions in other trees, they are very few. The sequoia heartwood, the *duramen*, the oldest wood in the tree, although in one sense dead, is always the hardest and soundest wood in the whole structure. This is a wonderful fact. These sequoias are sustained by a combination of the elements of soil, water, sunlight, and sun-heat, not to speak at all of the sustenance they, in common with all trees, derive from the nourishing air. The quality and continuity of this nourishment result in a height and girth that are astonishing. But in this respect the sequoias are not alone; the sugar-pine almost rivals them in stature, but falls far below them in bulk and age. The sugar-pines, too, are subject to many diseases; they therefore decay and die, while the most distinguishing and remarkable feature of the sequoias is, that not one of them, as far as observed, is subject to any disease. It is possible that this is partly due to the fact that they have greater sap-distributing (that is, life-giving) power than any other tree whatever. On this subject, Marsh says:

"In trees affected by no discoverable cause of death, decay begins at the topmost branches, which seem to wither and die for want of nutriment. The mysterious force by which the sap is carried to the roots, to the utmost twigs, cannot be conceived to be unlimited in power, and it is probable that it differs in different species; so that, while it may suffice to raise the fluid to the height of five hundred feet in the sequoia, it may not be able to carry it beyond one hundred and fifty feet in the oak. . . . Whenever a tree attains to the limit beyond which its circulating fluids cannot rise, we may suppose that death begins."

That limit has never been reached by the most gigantic sequoias now growing, and it is quite probable that, because of the perfection of their nourishment, they have equal perfection in the distribution of their sap. For what we know of the living sequoia we are almost wholly indebted to Mr. John Muir, the only man in the world who has made a prolonged botanical, personal study of them in their mountain homes.

Professor Asa Gray prophesied that the fossil remains of these trees would be found in the Arctic Circle. Nordenskjöld and others subsequently found these remains in great abundance there. Professor Gray says:

"The difference between the two big trees of California is as noticeable as their resemblance and their isolation. They are the survivors of a numerous family of wide distribution, which is first recognized in the cretaceous formation in several species, and which reached its maximum in middle tertiary in fourteen recognizable species or forms. Almost from the first, these separated into two groups, one foreshadowing the coast, the other the Sierra, redwood. The intermediate species are extinct, the two extreme forms have survived. . . . So the sequoias are of ancient stock ; their ancestors and kindreds formed a large part of the forest which flourished about the polar regions, and which extended into the low latitudes of Europe. . . . *Libocedrus* (the Incense Cedar), appears to have passed its lot with the sequoias. Two species, according to Heer, were with them in Spitzbergen. *Libocedrus decurrens* is one of the noblest associates of the present redwoods. But all the rest are in the southern hemisphere—two in the southern extremities of the Andes, two in the South Sea Islands. Pines of the same species, now found associated with the big trees, were then their associates in Greenland.''

How much is yet to be learned about these trees may be understood from the little we can say definitely about them in points herein mentioned. Could the sequoias be protected from fire, lightning, and storms, we would probably find trees, not one to four thousand years old, but of an age only to be reckoned from the far distant past, when they were first naturally sown in their last, present, and very limited habitat.

In reference to the age of these trees, Professor Alfred Russel Wallace lately wrote:

" Very absurd statements are made to visitors as to the antiquity of these trees, three or four thousand years

being usually given as their age. This is founded on the
fact that, while many of the large sequoias are greatly
damaged by fire, the large pines and firs around them are
quite uninjured. As many of these pines are assumed to
be near a thousand years old, the epoch of the 'great
fire' is supposed to be earlier still, and as the sequoias
have not outgrown the fire-scars in all that time, they are
supposed to have then arrived at their full growth. But
the simple explanation of these trees alone having suffered so much from fire, is that their bark is unusually
thick, dry, soft, and fibrous, and it thus catches fire more
easily and burns more readily and for a longer time than
that of the other *Coniferæ.* Forest fires occur continu-
ally, and the visible damage done to these trees has probably all occurred in the present century. Professor C. B.
Bradley, of the University of California, has carefully
counted the rings of annual growth on the stump of the
'Pavilion Tree,' and found them to be one thousand two
hundred and forty; and, after considering all that has
been alleged as to the uncertainty of this mode of esti-
mating the age of a tree, he believes that, in the climate
of California, in the zone of altitude where these trees
grow, the seasons of growth and repose are so strongly
marked that the number of annual rings gives an accurate result.   Other points that have been studied by
Professor Bradley are, the reasons why there are so few
young trees in the groves, and what is the cause of destruction of the old trees.   To take the last point first,
these noble trees seem to be singularly free from disease
or from decay due to old age.   All the trees that have
been cut down are solid to the heart, and none of the
standing trees show any indications of natural decay.
The only apparent cause of their overthrow is the wind;
and by noting the direction of a large number of fallen
trees it is found that the great majority of them lie more
or less toward the south. This is not the direction of the
prevalent winds, but many of the tallest trees lean toward
the south, owing to the increased growth of the topmost

branches toward the sun; they are then acted upon by violent gales, which loosen their roots, and whatever the direction of the wind that finally overthrows them, they fall in the direction of the over-balancing top weight.

"The young trees grow spiry and perfectly upright, but as soon as they overtop the surrounding trees and get the full influence of the sun and wind, the highest branches grow out laterally, killing those beneath their shade, and thus a dome-shaped top is produced. Taking into consideration the health and vigor of the largest trees, it seems probable that, under favorable conditions of shelter from violent winds and from a number of trees around them of nearly equal height, big trees might be produced far surpassing in height and bulk any that have yet been discovered."

If Professor Wallace, by personal examination and study, had arrived at the above conclusions, his knowledge and reputation would be the strongest possible guarantee of their correctness; but all he says was gathered from Professor Bradley, an associate professor of English in the University of California. Professor Bradley is not a botanist, and is neither here nor elsewhere recognized as an authority on the subject of the sequoias. How, indeed, could he be, since he never made any pretense of long personal study of either their age, growth, homes, or surroundings. He counted the rings of but one tree.

The sequoias are the coniferous tree kings of the earth. They possess, too, a striking individuality and nobility, more remarkable in

some respects than any of their other features.
They are surpassed in size only by two varie-
ties of the broad-leafed eucalyptus species of
Australia. The *Eucalyptus amygdalina* has
been seen four hundred and eighty feet in
height, and with a circumference of over one
hundred feet three feet from the ground, and
of eighty feet fifty-six feet from the surface.

Since California was settled our sequoias
have been subject to constant destruction and
vandalism by fire and the axe. Even their in-
fantile children were destroyed. If fire spared
them — which it never does — sheep, more
injurious to young trees than all other agents
of destruction combined, have for thirty years
been let loose in these magnificent and immortal groves, and each of them, whether the
young of one year or the king of four thousand
years, were alike doomed to destruction from
the various causes enumerated.

The war with these trees and their pine,
cedar, and fir companions is a war against
unsurpassed size, grace, strength, beauty, maj-
esty, and comparatively everlasting age. The
United States Government, until lately, was
utterly unworthy of the heritage of them.
That ruin and desolation would follow their
loss was never denied; and yet all that was

said and written on this subject, and all the
analogies cited from the experience of numerous countries where forest denudation has produced the most widespread soil and climatic
desolation and disaster, fell until lately upon
unhearing official ears.   But Mr. Noble, Secre-
tary of the Interior under President Harrison's
administration, determined thoroughly to in-
vestigate this forest question, in which he was
ably aided by the Sierra Club (of which Mr.
John Muir was President), and by all parties
interested in irrigation, which depends *wholly*
in this State on the rivers of the Sierra Nevada,
and they, in their turn, are nearly wholly dependent on forest preservation.   Mr. Noble sent
two commissioners to the Sierra Nevada, whose
reports revealed almost innumerable cases of
bold-faced forest robbery under the dummy
system of perjury and land-grabbing.   Their
report also showed the vital need of the im-
mediate ejection of sheep and cattle from the
mountains in summer.   Their owners for
thirty years have enjoyed free pasture there.
Here, as in Europe, it has been abundantly
shown that pasturage, especially of sheep, even
where it did not cause herders' fires, was utterly destructive to the natural condition of the
always friable soil and to all shrubbery and

young trees. The shrubbery as much as the
large trees serves as a shade and protection for
snow. It is an efficient sunshade, detaining
the snow in its summer tendency of hasty return to the freedom of water.

The commissioners referred to, recommend-
ed that the size of the Yosemite reservation,
containing nearly one million acres, be not
reduced. A California Congressman (Mr.
Caminetti) has been laboring assiduously for
its reduction, on the ground that a number of
miners and settlers will be treated unjustly if
the reservation is preserved intact. Acting upon
thorough information thus personally obtained
by Mr. Noble's commissioners, and upon the
latter's strong recommendation, President Harrison, by virtue of power conferred on him by
an act of Congress of 1893, reserved all of the
western slope of the Sierra Nevada range from
private entry, from the Yosemite National Park
on the north to the southern extremity of the
range, thus protecting the head-waters of all
the streams tributary to the great San Joaquin
Valley. This measure was by far the greatest boon conferred on California by President
Harrison's administration. But the work is
not complete. President Cleveland should
finish it by reserving the other half of the

Sierra Nevada, from the Yosemite Park to the Oregon line. Mr. Muir thinks that all the great forest belts of this coast should be under the control of the General Government forever. But neither Oregon nor Washington need irrigation.

That portion of the forests of the Sierra still left in Government ownership is so only because of its inaccessibility. All timber lands worth two dollars and a half an acre have been appropriated, to an elevation of about six thousand feet. Those higher up, and subject still to reservation, will in many cases not remain long so. Wagon-roads or railroads, by making them accessible, will make them worth stealing; that being the word expressive of the nearly universal means by which " Uncle Sam " has been despoiled of the most magnificent coniferous woods on the face of the earth. Too soon — all too soon — they are destroyed or stolen; but they will never, alas, never return! Long-drawn centuries were required for their growth, and as long-stretching years would be needed for their replacement; but the fact is, that when once cut, or otherwise destroyed, they will *never* be replaced. With their removal all the requisites of soil protection and moisture will be changed. The Sierra, with them, has the most glorious forests on the face of the earth; without them, as in all such cases of denudation, blistered, bare rocks and soils, torn by short-lived spring torrents, carrying sand, mud, rocks, and desolation to the valleys below, will succeed. The completion of the reservation of the whole Sierra Nevada northward cannot be too speedily included in Mr. Harrison's reservation of the southern half. This business of reserving forests is a case of the *most pressing, most vital necessity*, not on behalf of California alone, but of all the other arid States—Nevada, Utah, Arizona, New Mexico, Idaho, and Colorado. But this last is a subject upon which I cannot here enter, although it is a pressing and most mournful one. California's case is the most important, only because the trees to be saved are far the largest and the finest of their species in the world. So far, too, as Colorado is concerned, there is little left for the Government to save. Railroad builders, charcoal burners, cattlemen, sheepherders, and lumbermen have already swept off nearly all of the comparatively small and sparsely growing forests of that State.

Another persistent effort is just now being made to reduce the size of the Yosemite timber reservation described, on the plea that honest settlers' rights will suffer; that there is irrigable land on some portions of the tract, and that there are also mineral lands on it. Let the settlers, if there are any honest ones there, be recompensed, but under no circumstances should the reserve be reduced. Any change in it, no matter how disguised, means its reopening to timber-grabbers, and the destruction of its forests.

Wealth and Poverty of the Chicago Exposition.

Wealth and Poverty of the Chicago Exposition.

THE World's Fair at Chicago was a greater Exposition than that last held at Paris, as the Paris Exposition was greater than the preceding one at Philadelphia. Each of these Expositions, indeed, is greater — necessarily greater — than its predecessor, simply because each is carrying more time, and with more time more advance in the progressive, as compared with the stationary arts. Of the latter, I especially mean those arts which have mental expression only, poetry and the drama, and by the progressive arts, those which demand both mental invention and physical expression — sculpture, architecture, painting, music, and mechanics. Men's minds have not ceased to labor in the greatest of the arts first named — that is, in poetry and the drama, — and work has been performed in both within the last half century which is worthy of both deep study and of high praise; yet small approach to equaling, much less surpassing, the poetry or drama of past ages can now be registered. Indeed, Shakespeare, Homer, Æschylus, Euripides, Sophocles, Aristophanes,

Virgil and Horace, Dante and Milton, and
to some minds Goethe and Schiller, Molière
and Racine also, as poets and dramatists,
tragic or comic, and as moralists, philosophers,
naturalists, sages and wits, have so exhausted
human admiration, and so closely attained to
perfection, that there seems little real foothold
left for their successors. However admirable
the latter may have been, and however much
read or praised their works may be, it is
still generally felt, after the expression of
all praise, that they are hardly in the list
with the "poets paramount" who so long ago
preceded them. As Hazlitt has said: "The
niches are occupied; the tables are full."

The world is so thoroughly explored, that,
omitting science, probably nearly all of what,
in a strictly literary sense, is known as learning has been revealed. The shackles have
for ages been taken from the human mind,
and legal obstacles withdrawn from all human
effort. We therefore can hardly imagine
another age like the golden one of Greece,
or the mental triumphs, in a book sense, of
that of Elizabeth. The conviction is some-
what similar, but not nearly so strong, in
regard to sculpture, architecture, and painting.
Few believe it possible that a mind and age-

encircling genius like Shakespeare can again appear, unless by some world-transforming scientific discovery, or new mental revolution far surpassing anything now likely to occur. Puck's promise of putting a girdle around the earth in forty minutes — then apparently as light, airy, and fabulous as the play in which it occurs — has long ago been more than realized; and even its comparative performance, as a fact of human transportation, either in the air or through the earth, would not now in some respects be as wonderful as was the defeat of the Persians, the birth of a new sense of Hellenic nationality, and the opening up of the Old World to observation and increased colonization by the Greeks, or the discoveries of the treasures of the old learning, the breaking up of ecclesiasticism, the substitution of the Copernican for the Ptolemaic system of astronomy, and the discovery of a new world, were to the Continent and England of the time of Elizabeth. In sculpture and architecture, Egypt, originally, had great influence upon Greece; and Italy, in learning, had a similar influence upon England.

Probably no nation can experience more than one such climacteric as that which the Greece of Pericles, the Italy of Lorenzo, and the England of Elizabeth experienced. The events which created those periods were world-transforming in their importance. They affected every human interest, mental and physical. Beside these, the three most memorable epochs in the world's history, the late terrible struggle which resulted in the unification of Germany, or the War of the Rebellion, which first solidly cemented the Great Republic, was a comparatively unimportant event. In each of these cases the struggle and the results were of tremendous importance; but each was but a great episode, and not an epoch, in the history of the nation passing through it. Each was a physical and national, only partially mental, and not at all a world-embracing, new birth. In proof of this, attention may be called to the fact that the literature of neither nation was profoundly affected, and therefore was not transformed by these events.

The writer does not think of asserting that the nineteenth century has been barren of great poets and prose writers. The fact, indeed, is that the *general* contributions to literature of the past half-century have never been surpassed, in either quantity or quality. Whatever poverty the nineteenth century has exhibited in poetry is relative only. That is, it is poor only when compared to the works of the few poets — the concentrated geniuses of all the ages — already named. But leaving these, and these only, aside, Tennyson's "In Memoriam" and "Princess," and Longfellow's "Evangeline" and "Keramos," will bear comparison with the works of any other poets of any other age whatever. Whittier's "Snow Bound," not equal to Gray's "Elegy" or Burns' "Cotter's Saturday Night," is still worthy, as simple annals of the New England poor at their hospitable firesides, to be placed beside those great pastorals, both in a poetical and heart-touching sense. Macaulay, Motley, and Fiske, as philosophic, graphic, and brilliant writers of history, have seldom been surpassed in any age; while for double gifts as an essayist, De Quincey has never been equaled. As a writer of spiritualized English of the most weird and heart-stirring power, he is seen at his best in his "Confessions of an Opium Eater." Brilliant with high color as his word-painting there is, it never oversteps good taste or chastity of description. Common - sense guides his pen, even when he describes opium dreams and hallucinations. His language, though like his dreams — gorgeous, — is never

more extravagant than an attempt at full
description necessitates; while, on the other
hand, for the qualities of gentle humor, deli-
cate fancy, and the most subtle wit, he is seen
at his best in "Murder as a Fine Art." The
best touches of Charles Lamb and Washington Irving are not equal to that essay of De
Quincey's.

Other ages, too, cannot, because natural
science is so recent, pretend to furnish such
graceful prose-writing, illustrating scientific
truth, as that of Tyndall and Huxley. English is there exhibited in a dual capacity, at
its best in direct force, power and scientific
accuracy, with imagery and description of the
most appropriate poetic beauty and felicity.
If the works of Darwin, Wallace, Agassiz, and
Draper are referred to last, it is not because
they are least. These naturalists have made
the results of their study of outdoor nature
as intensely interesting as the most brillant
novel, sober fact being illuminated with the
most wonderful scientific theoretical general-
izations, which, but that they *are* facts, would
be relegated to the airy regions of fancy.
The poor earthworm, on which we had pre-
viously heedlessly trampled, was shown by
Darwin almost to deserve deification, for its

universal and almost miraculous service to agriculture.

If, therefore, the student who has confined himself to and made the best poetical and prose writers of the nineteenth century his own, cannot, as he must not, boast that he has drunk at the deepest well-springs, especially of poetic thought, he can at least boast (the limits before prescribed being still prominently remembered), of having indulged in not less fine, while more varied, intellectual nourishment than any age of the world has hitherto been capable of providing.

When we take what comes next to authorship, the arts that address themselves to both the mental and physical eye, we are, it is true, in a still very lofty, but yet a lower, world. *Therefore*, it is still believed to be possible at least, that such sculptors and architects as the unknown Egyptian sculptors of Abou Simel, the architects of Karnak, or such Greek sculptors or architects as Phidias, Praxiteles, Ictinus, and Lysippus; such Italian sculptors as Brunelleschi, Bramante, Sansovino, Michel Angelo, Omodeo, and Lombardi; such painters as Michel Angelo, Raphael, Leonardo da Vinci, Correggio, Fra Angelico, Perugino, Titian, Salvator Rosa, Tintoretto, Van Dyck, and Rubens; the Gothic architecture of the cathedral of Amiens, Rheims, Salisbury, and Cologne, or the Romanesque Gothic of Milan, may all yet be surpassed. There has not, it is true, since those artists' days been any very hopeful sign that this will occur; but it is not regarded, as it is in the case of the work of the poets and dramatists paramount, as almost impossible. Therefore, whatever was exhibited at the Chicago Exposition — the great poets' works, necessarily, not being on exhibition there — for study in architecture, sculpture, and painting, were but copies in some shape of the work of the giants of the olden days, the works of men who have nestled in their brains and therefrom borrowed their ideas. The value of all latter-day work, indeed, is largely measured by its success in keeping the great masters in mind. All later laborers, not excepting the greatest of them (in sculpture), Thorwaldsen and Canova, are but copyists, and not improvements on those who preceded them. The giant in the plastic arts who will in genius and execution surpass the ultimate attainments of the old masters, may be possible, but he has not yet appeared, nor is he very sanguinely looked for. In his "Short History of Art," Turner asserts that from the eastern frieze of the Parthenon more is to be learnt of the true principles of art than from all the books that have ever been written. Ruskin, quoted and endorsed by Symonds, says: "This is the simple test, then, of a perfect school — that it has represented the human form so that it is impossible to conceive of its being better done. And that, I repeat, has been accomplished twice only — once in Athens, and once in Florence."

On this subject, W. J. Stillman, the art critic, says:

"No one can admit that the human intellect is weaker than it was five or twenty centuries ago; but it is certain that if we take the pains to study what was done five centuries ago in painting, or twenty centuries ago in sculpture, and compare it with the best work of to-day, we shall find the latter trivial and 'prentice work compared with the ordinary work of men whose names are lost in the lustre of a school. The distinction is not one of mental caliber — for now and then we see arise an individual of as strong and marked an artistic mind as any but the two or three supreme men of the past; but their best work (and none are more willing than they to admit it) is but amateurs' accomplishment beside the certainty and comprehensiveness, both in vision and execution, of even minor masters of the great time. . . . There is not one living painter who can paint a portrait as a Venetian painter of A. D. 1550 would have done it; only one, in my knowledge, who has the same feeling for it. If we go to the work of wider range, the Campo Santo of Pisa, the Stanze, the Sistine Chapel, the distance becomes an abyss; the simplest

fragment of a Greek statue of B. C. 450 shows us that
the best sculpture of this century, even the French, is
only a happy child-work, not even to be put in sight of
Donatello or Michel Angelo.

For these reasons, in these directions, the
Chicago Exposition did not nearly equal the
first London Exhibition of 1851. But in other
respects the late Exposition surpassed all of
its predecessors. This advance is mostly in
what we may term the utilitarian arts, and in
practical science, towards perfection in which
the most of the genius of the nineteenth century has been and is still running, since the
great authors of the past so triumphed that it
is felt no present effort can equal, much less
surpass, its achievements. The triumphs of the
world now are mostly in the mechanical arts;
and poetry — we say, *poetry* — of a very high
character is being wrought in and expressed
by them. This assertion may at first sight be
doubted; but a practically unanimous verdict
for it can be obtained, we think, by calling attention to a few facts. Let us take one of the
first locomotives, — the "Rocket" of Stephenson, — first run on rails in England in 1830.
That primitive machine is simply, in general
outline and construction, a rough engine and
boiler, stuck rudely on boards and wheels. To
the mental and physical eye of even the person

most ignorant of mechanics, it is an utterly clumsy and inefficient machine; how much more so, therefore, to the educated mechanic. Place it beside a locomotive of to-day, and the difference in power and speed of the two machines is not greater than their difference in appearance. The difference is as great as that between a child's comical drawing of the human figure and a like sketch by a skilled artist. Yet Stephenson's rough-looking boiler on boards and rude wheels was the parent of the present locomotive. The change is so vast, however, in the development of grace, beauty, strength, compactness of build, and intense concentrated propelling energy, as to be really a new creation. In these points, indeed, as a world-transforming means of land transportation, that small vehicle, the English locomotive, has no peer. The American locomotive is equally powerful, but it is not so small, simple, or compact. When we compare the progress thus made, we cannot help seeing that beauty, strength, concentration of power, ease of motion, and therefore grace, have been continuous. Harmony in the highest mechanical expression has consequently elicited poetry from this utilitarian means of land transportation.

Of the English locomotive Ruskin says: " I cannot express the amazed awe, the crushed humility with which I sometimes watch a locomotive take its breath at a railway station, and think what work there is in its bars and wheels, and what manner of men they must be who dig brown ironstone out of the ground and forge it into *that*. What assemblage of accurate and mighty faculties in them, . . . infinitely complex anatomy of active steel, compared with which the skeleton of a living creature would seem to a careless observer clumsy and vile." This from Ruskin, who frequently berated steam, smoke, and factories as blots on the landscape, insisting that water-power factories only should be tolerated.

And yet, true as this illustration is in the case of the locomotive, moving over hill and valley at lightning speed, it does not afford anything like as fine an illustration of mechanical art progress, moving forward in physical harmony and poetry, as it increases in size, power, concentration, usefulness, and speed, as the ocean steamship offers. The rigid rail affords little opportunity for display of grace and ease of motion, compared to the undulatory freedom of movement possible in water. The Cunard Steamship Company had on exhibition at Chicago a complete and beautiful model of the first steamship of the line, the *Britannia*, which crossed the Atlantic in 1840, in fourteen days and eight hours, with steam and sail power. She was of eleven hundred and fifty-four tons, and seven hundred and forty horse-power. Her cargo capacity was two hundred and twenty-five tons. She had a length of two hundred and seven feet, a breadth of beam of thirty-four and a third feet, and a depth of twenty-four and a third feet. The company had also models of the other side-wheelers in use, until they were succeeded by propellers. Beside these models, is that of the latest triumph of marine engineering, the mammoth *Campania*, of twelve thousand nine hundred and fifty tons burden, and thirty thousand horse-power. Her length is six hundred and twenty feet, her breadth of beam sixty-five and a quarter feet, and depth of hold forty-three feet. Looking at these various steps of progress in marine architecture, the most ignorant can see at a glance, that the increased power, size, speed, carrying capacity, and passenger comfort of the *Campania* do not more surpass the *Britannia* than the grace, beauty of lines, and general appearance of the former vessel do those of the latter. The tendency evidently has been, and is, to greater length, less breadth of beam and depth of hull, to rounded and keelless bottoms — in other words, to greater litheness, more fast-swimming, fish-like shape, and therefore to much greater avoidance of contest with water and wave resistance. Nor can it be claimed that these changes resulted in less strength, safety in sea-going qualities, or more stomach discomfort from rolling and pitching. Anything like a full appreciation of vessels like the *Campania* and *Paris* can not be had unless a few facts are recited: The very largest land engines in factories are only of about two thousand horse-power, and the largest locomotives have only two hundred to three hundred; the *Campania* is of thirty thousand and the *Paris* of twenty thousand horse-power. No one knows what great mechanical energy is who has not been in the engine-rooms of these vessels while under full headway. The power and rapidity of motion of the engines of the *Paris* can only be expressed by saying that they are illustrations of tremendous mechanical fury in action; and the wonder, after thus seeing them, is not that the vessel runs so fast, but that she does not run much faster. This is accounted for by air, wind,

and water resistance. Yet lying-to in even
a North Atlantic winter tempest is now practically out of date. These vessels, and those
of the other crack lines also, can uninterrupt-
edly stride over the most mountainous seas,
defy the fury of the wildest head gales, and
yet still speed on at the rate of three hundred
and fifty to four hundred miles a day — their
full rate of speed being five hundred to five
hundred and fifty miles. Their machinery
seems powerful enough almost to turn the
world, if ever it should grow tired of revolv-
ing on its axis. The fires in the boilers seem
large and numerous enough to form a Tophet,
in point of size and heat. The *Campania* has
one hundred and two furnaces. These are
probably the largest fires ever kindled by man
on the earth, and the wide-throated blasts of
draught let in on them keep them up to a rage
of white heat at all times.

The Cramps of Philadelphia have just finished the first of two steamships for the American line. These vessels will, in speed at least,
it is promised, surpass the *Campania*, *Lucania*,
and *Paris*. The *Campania* has forty times the
power of the *Britannia*, but uses only five times
the fuel. Either the *Campania* or *Paris* can
carry as many passengers on one trip as the

first four ships of the Cunard line could have carried in a year.

Steamships of the type of the *Campania* of the Cunard line, and the *Paris* of the Inman line, and some of the vessels built by the Cramps of Philadelphia, are such monsters in size, power, and carrying capacity, and yet such perfect models of speed, grace, and beauty, because of their harmony of lines, length of hulls, and seabird ease of sitting the water, that the most stolid beholder would at once admit that these magnificent vessels —"which o'er green Neptune's back of ships make cities"—are literally epic poems on the water—poems which their architects built for utility, but which have almost greater grace and beauty than utility. And the great marine architect could not avoid, consciously or unconsciously, thus running in lines of grace, although his most ardent intent was increased power, carrying capacity, strength, and speed. Progress in these great utilitarian means of land and ocean transport has all been toward vastly greater ease of motion, beauty, and harmony, and therefore grace and poetry — a poetry visible and perfectly appreciable, as I have said, to even the uneducated eye. The same facts will be found in all of our factories — perhaps not so plainly visible, because the machinery in them is not detached and moving in the same graceful, enclosing vehicles as a locomotive on land or a steamship in the water.

The present saving in fuel is most notable, too. The old steamships consumed five pounds of coal per horse-power per hour; the new marine racers but one and a half pounds. In the old engines, steam was used but once; now it does duty three to four times, by triple or quadruple expansion engines. Instead of the old pressure of thirty pounds, one hundred and fifty to one hundred and eighty pounds are used; steel instead of iron boilers make this great pressure consistent with safety. The machinery and boilers are all proportionately lighter and much less complicated.

Now, after the relation of these facts of mechanical art progress, and the assertion, which will not be disputed, that the world has not recently achieved such triumphs in strictly literary work, or in sculpture, architecture, and painting as it did in past ages, it is time to ask if it must in the future content itself with the development of mechanical grace with utility — with poetry and power in the locomotive and the steamship, in the factory and

in the field, rather than the very highest triumphs that have ever been recorded in poetry,
painting, sculpture, or architecture? We answer, that this seems probable, and not only
probable, but reasonable, if the amelioration
of the condition of the world's workers is to
continue. The Golden Age is still far off; yet
the present age is a very forward one compared with the past. The steamship and
locomotive, either originally or in their im-
provement, have helped the world forward
immensely. They have not wholly or nearly
abolished poverty. That is true, indeed; yet
the age, *with* them, has taken many steps in
that direction. The world has improved very
much indeed within the last half century.
Mechanical invention has been the instrument
and means of an exceedingly large proportion
of this advance. Without rapid transportation, little progress could be made in the
amelioration of the condition of the poor.
Bad as the condition of the small farmer or
agricultural laborer may now be, in consequence of the vastly increased world competi-
tion caused by the far greater rapidity of ocean
and land transportation, neither of them is
anything like as badly off as he was fifty
years ago. In other words, let the list of com-

plaints against the present age be ever so long and weighty, no one dreams that they could be lessened by a return to the comparatively near past. Very few European laborers now work for six or eight cents a day, while that sum was a common rate of wages everywhere half a century ago. No Scotch peasant has now the hard time that Burns and his father experienced in scraping together the barest necessities of life as small farmers. India has been saved from periodical and unavoidable seasons of famine, not by philanthropy so much as by railroad lines. Without the latter the strongest philanthropy or the most liberal charity could not aid, because it could not in time reach the suffering. The Yellow River and its overflow are still China's sorrow, by creating periodical famines, because Chinese stolidity and unprogressiveness will not tolerate railroads.

In the comparative infancy of railroads, in 1856, Robert Stephenson asserted that the railroads of Great Britain then effected a direct annual saving of forty million pounds sterling (two hundred millions of dollars). This sum, he said, exceeded by about fifty per cent. the interest on the National debt. The present railroads of that country cost over nine hundred millions of pounds sterling, or say four billion five hundred million dol- lars. If all railroads were obliterated in the United States, the property, personal and landed, of the whole country would be reduced at once one-half, if not two-thirds. And yet steam is but an inefficient industrial tool. About eighty-five per cent. of the heat of coal is lost in turning it into working energy in the steam-engine. But before this loss is modified or wholly corrected, the world, by electricity or some other mode of creating power, will probably have advanced in mechanics to a higher, faster, and far more effective agent than steam power by land and sea. Coal, of course, will still be needed in the production of electrical power.

The continued amelioration of the sufferings and hardships of the common people of the world can confidently be looked for from the continued progress of the mechanical arts. They have been and will continue in a much higher degree to be expressions of and ministers to utility, philanthropy and poetry. Look, for instance, at the progress made through gang and steam plows, reapers, and harvesters. The man who now sits comfortably driving a gang plow seems out more for a pleasant day's drive and airing than a day's hard work, and the same is measurably true of the changed modes of reaping and threshing. The worst hand drudgery of plowing, reaping, and threshing has passed away, on the large farms of the United States at least. Thirty steam threshers only were required to prepare for market the wheat crop of two counties in Ohio, which would otherwise have required the labor of forty thousand men. These are the lines in which the genius of the world is running; these the tablets on which it is recording both its material and mental expression and progress, and inscribing its poetry also. This is the "New Learning" of Bacon, in utilitarian shape, but still in unquestioned wisdom and poetic expression. Perhaps some scholar in his closet, classicist in his study, or worshiper of sculpture, architecture, and painting will mourn and lament over all of this. But, as they have been the very persons who most strongly and continuously iterated and reiterated the truth upon our remembrance, that these masters of the past cannot possibly be equaled, and, as a rule, but faintly imitated, in the present, perhaps they are partially to blame for turning a portion of the current of the world's genius to fields in which it has achieved incomparable triumphs — triumphs, too, in which progress is certain to continue to be still more rapid and assured. "What, then," said Macaulay, in his essay on Bacon, "was the end which Bacon proposed to himself? It was, to use his own emphatic expression, *fruit*. It was the multiplying of human enjoyments and the mitigation of human suffering. It was the relief of man's estate." No Exposition in the world ever exhibited such an array of machines and appliances for the relief of humanity and the mitigation of prostrating drudgery, and therefore for "the relief of man's estate," as that at Chicago. It pointed, too, to a day, not far distant, when machinery will still more effectually, and far more cheaply, lighten the burdens of humanity, and transport man by land and sea, and probably through the air, with far greater rapidity. The words of Macaulay inscribed over the Transportation Building at Chicago may be quoted, illustrative of the truths we have been here recording: "Of all inventions, the alphabet and printing-press alone excepted, those which have served to abridge distance have been most useful to civilization." The triumphs of electricity will almost certainly far surpass those of steam.

It is the coming giant of greater speed and power. By it steam will be vanquished, though not abolished, for it is needed to produce electricity. And since human effort could not compete successfully with past art and genius, it was very natural that it should strike for lines in which it could be regnant, and where the amelioration of the condition of humanity will attain its chief triumphs. Let not the fact be forgotten either, that with great mechanical there has also been vast mental progress. This combination has been so great, and the union so fruitful, that the combined product renders this the greatest mental and material age the world has ever seen.

Note, too, that a higher science than that embraced in the very highest branches of mechanical art has been directly, or indirectly, constantly laboring for, and aiding, that art on all sides. We allude to natural philosophy and the pure science connected therewith. The most notable laborers in England in this field have been Faraday, Joule, Thomson, Huxley, and Tyndall, with Draper and Edison in America. These great investigators in the practical sciences, especially in the departments of chemistry and electricity, have made dis-

coveries as ethereal and poetical as anything
in the Midsummer Night's Dream or the Tempest, while at the same time founded, as the
magnificent "airy nothings" of these works
are not, on immovable pillars of solid fact.
Michael Faraday was one of the best repre-
sentatives of these scientists. Their hands
and experiments were on the earth, but their
thoughts and imaginations ranged almost to
heaven. It is no exaggeration to say that
even Shakespeare himself would have been
honored by Faraday's company. Certainly,
Faraday soared to and labored in as high a
heaven of invention. To the scientist of the
nineteenth century, as to the poets of *all* centuries, nature is but the sensible expression of
the spiritual. His crucibles, machines, and
tools may seem very mechanical and coarse
instruments of research; but through them,
aided and elevated by the highest powers of
the imagination, he has revealed truths on
which the mind finds a repose productive of
the greatest intellectual joy and content.
When we perceive and admit this, then "all
dregs and sediments," as Symonds says, in
another sense, "of the analytical, mechanical
alembic sink to the bottom, leaving a clear,
crystalline elixir of the spirit." The men who

have soared the highest in the scientific sky, too, have not worked for gain. They had their pay in their work — a wealth that the world knows not of,— in their consultations with nature, and their joy in the laurels from the temple of industrial peace with which their brows were crowned.

After long labor in the mysterious field of the Correlation of the Forces, Faraday said: "I have long held an opinion, almost amounting to conviction, in common, I believe, with many other lovers of natural knowledge, that the various forms under which the forces of matter are made manifest have one common origin, or, in other words, are so directly related and mutually dependent that they are convertible, as it were, one into another, and possess equivalents of power in their action."

Commenting on this theory, Tyndall says: "Faraday's difficulty in dealing with these conceptions was at bottom the same as that of Newton — that he was, in fact, trying to overleap this difficulty, and with it probably the limits prescribed to the intellect itself." Yet, Tyndall adds: "In his search for the unity of all force, he made all his great discoveries. The discovery of magneto-electricity is the

greatest experimental result ever obtained by
an investigator." In speaking of the importance and usefulness of the metals, Faraday
said that "refined civilization would be impossible without them." He also said that
"the ancients deified them for a far more re-
stricted use." What a pleasure it is to remember that the assertion was justly made of this
great physicist "that his life was a struggle
always to say that which he thought was true,
and to do that which he thought was kind."
It was said by Sir David Brewster of Sir Isaac
Newton's "Principia," that it was a work that
might be carried to other worlds, and find its
truths there as solid and acceptable as on this
speck of earth. Much of Faraday's work was
of a like character.

The nineteenth century, therefore, with such
explorers and conquerors in the highest intellectual realms of physical truth — the fruit
of their labors nearly all consisting of mechanical art triumphs — is not poor, but rich beyond computation. Those men, though laborers in a different field, were justly comparable
to the greatest poets, architects, sculptors and
painters the world has ever seen.

Considered from a practical and poetical
point of view, there never was such an

Exposition as that of Chicago. Every civilized country placed there its masterpieces of
mechanical art progress; and if we can imagine the goddess of civilization and humanity presiding there, she must have trium-
phantly exclaimed, as she looked over the
miraculous machines: "These are my jewels."

And there is another and more poetical
side to these utilitarian Expositions. Emer-
son expressed it. He said that the real ship
is the *mind* of the ship-builder. Therefore,
although expressed in material ships, locomotives, and gigantic or microscopic machines,
to the student by far the most wonderful
sights revealed in that Exposition were the
expressions of the minds of the inventors,
and the physicists, their leaders and allies; and,
therefore, those best capable of appreciating
them were there as much *alone with the mind*
as with Shakespeare in Hamlet, Macbeth, or
the Tempest, with Michel Angelo in the Sistine Chapel or in the dome of St. Peter's.
Imagination, therefore, still rules the world.
Of all the children of genius, indeed, though
gifted with very different mental gifts and
expressions, it may be said, quoting the
Psalmist, "I have said ye are gods, and *all
of you* children of the Most High." In many

cases, too, as great mental agony, suffering, isolation, and want of world appreciation would be revealed, if the history of all these machines and their progress could be read, as Shakespeare, Dante, and Michel Angelo endured. Every great genius, indeed, in any department of supreme human effort, is at some period, and frequently all his life, "a man of sorrows and acquainted with grief," but his joy cometh in the morning of success; and the greatest and best of these men, but for the sustenance of ideas, could not have worked, endured and triumphed as they did. If the Chicago Exposition, therefore, was comparatively poor in what heretofore has been called the "fine" arts, it was rich beyond expression in those which are both utilitarian and ideal, in useful and demo-cratic blessings, the fruits of which all the sons and daughters of men may in some sort largely share. Is not, indeed, the miti-gation of human loads and labor the high-est poetry; the harnessing of the forces of nature to human use, progress in the great-est utility and divine harmony? Kepler's was a mind comparable perhaps only to Shakespeare's, in the elevation of the range of its imaginative element. If restored to this life, that "new Prometheus and heaven-scaler," as he was called, would have been an enraptured visitor at Chicago, and doubt-less would cheerfully have admitted that his work on Celestial Mechanics ("Harmonics of the World") might well be linked with ter-restrial harmonies, as illustrated by the tiny or Titanic mechanical triumphs there on ex-hibition, of which triumphs, too, this country can justly claim the largest share.